The Day Teddy Met Grubby

This story reminds us of our s
how they begin and hoy

Story by:
Ken Forsse

Illustrated by:
David High
Russell Hicks
Theresa Mazurek
Julie Armstrong
Allyn Conley/Gorniak

WORLDS OF WONDER™

ubby™   Newton Gimmick™   Princess Aruzia™   Leota™   Wooly What's-It™   Prince Arin™   Fobs™

My family lived in a
little cottage.

I was up that night seeing
if I could find any more of
those wonderful little roots.

I think we caught the potato thief.

And they pop right up
out of the ground
to find the morning sun.

Grubby and I had fun watching the potatoes and other vegetables sprout up out of the ground.

"Teddy Ruxpin is
My Friend"